The Dead Sea Squirrels Series

Squirreled Away
Boy Meets Squirrels
Nutty Study Buddies
Squirrelnapped!
Tree-mendous Trouble
Whirly Squirrelies
Merle of Nazareth
A Dusty Donkey Detour
Jingle Squirrels
Risky River Rescue

Jingle Squirrels

Mike Nawrocki

Illustrated by Luke Séguin-Magee

Tyndale House Publishers
Carol Stream, Illinois

Visit Tyndale's website for kids at tyndale.com/kids.

Visit the author's website at mikenawrocki.com.

Tyndale is a registered trademark of Tyndale House Ministries. The Tyndale Kids logo is a trademark of Tyndale House Ministries.

The Dead Sea Squirrels is a registered trademark of Michael L. Nawrocki.

Jingle Squirrels

Copyright © 2021 by Mike Nawrocki. All rights reserved.

Illustrations by Luke Séguin-Magee. Copyright © Tyndale House Ministries. All rights reserved.

Designed by Libby Dykstra

Edited by Deborah King

Published in association with the literary agency of Brentwood Studios, 1550 McEwen, Suite 300 PNB 17, Franklin, TN 37067.

Scripture quotations are taken from the *Holy Bible*, New Living Translation, copyright © 1996, 2004, 2015 by Tyndale House Foundation. Used by permission of Tyndale House Publishers, Carol Stream, Illinois 60188. All rights reserved.

Jingle Squirrels is a work of fiction. Where real people, events, establishments, organizations, or locales appear, they are used fictitiously. All other elements of the novel are drawn from the author's imagination.

For manufacturing information regarding this product, please call 1-855-277-9400.

For information about special discounts for bulk purchases, please contact Tyndale House Publishers at csresponse@tyndale.com, or call 1-855-277-9400.

Library of Congress Cataloging-in-Publication Data

A catalog record for this book is available from the Library of Congress.

ISBN 978-1-4964-4981-8

Printed in the United States of America

27	26	25	24	23	22	21
7	6	5	4	3	2	1

To Nona and Dennis, aka Mom and Dad:
I'm so grateful for your love and support over
the years and am especially thankful you
raised my brothers and me to love Jesus.

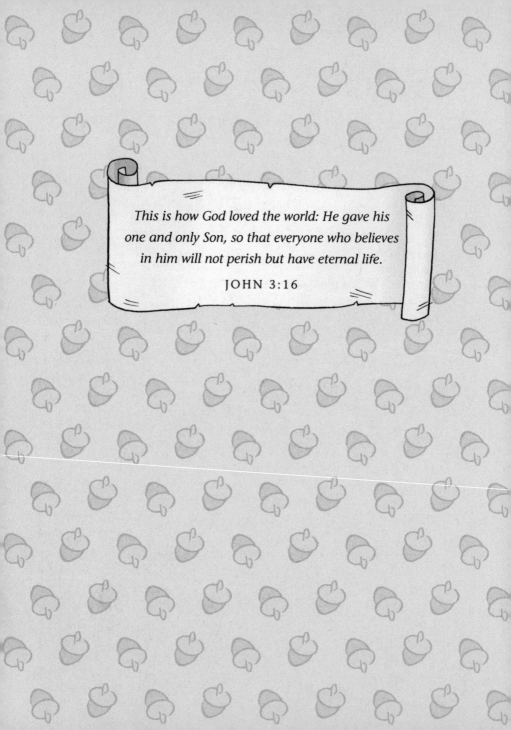

This is how God loved the world: He gave his one and only Son, so that everyone who believes in him will not perish but have eternal life.

JOHN 3:16

BUT WAIT!

BEFORE WE START...

Who are the Dead Sea Squirrels?

ISRAEL, AD 70 Merle and Pearl cruise down the Jordan River...

...on the vacation of a lifetime!

The squirrels end up at the Dead Sea, where...

You can't sink! I've always wanted to not sink!

Couldn't you have just worn your floaties in the lake back home?

Soon the two salty squirrels are hot, thirsty, and desperate for shade. Then they spot a cave.

If God wanted you to go into a cave, he would have made you a bat.

Merle's sense of adventure lures him into the cave, despite Pearl's protests.

Ten-year-old Michael Gomez is spending the summer at the Dead Sea with his professor dad and his best friend, Justin.

While exploring a cave (without his dad's permission), Michael discovers two dried-out, salt-covered critters and stashes them in his backpack.

Michael sneaks the squirrels back home with him to Tennessee.

He sets them up like posable action figures on his dresser—under an open window.

While Michael is sleeping, a thunderstorm rolls in, and it begins to rain . . .

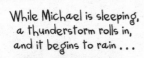

. . . rehydrating the squirrels!

Up and kicking again after almost 2,000 years, Merle and Pearl Squirrel have great stories and advice to share with the modern world.

They are the Dead Sea Squirrels!

But the Dead Sea Squirrels' adventures don't end there. Merle and Pearl soon find out that things are

a whole lot different

from the first century!

For one thing, there are self-filling fresh water bowls . . .

an endless supply of walnuts and chicken nuggets . . .

Thank you, chickens, for your nuggets!

and much fancier places to live!

I could get used to this!

Plus, they get to go to fifth grade (as long as no one sees them)!

Stay still, Merle! Pretend you are stuffed!

But even in quiet Walnut Creek, Tennessee, danger is never too far away!

Nice kitty...

What if Mom and Dad find out?!

And a man in a suit and sunglasses who wants nothing more than to get his hands on the squirrels ... does!

HELP!!!

Now it's back to the Holy Land to rescue the squirrels!

MICHAEL!

CHAPTER 1

An eighteen-pound turkey? Stuffing and cranberry sauce? The Gomez family gathering around a table on a cold, late-November afternoon with Mr. Nemesis licking mashed potatoes off of Jane's fingers?

"Did I miss the part where the squirrels were rescued and brought back to Tennessee just in time for Thanksgiving?" you might be thinking.

"I WISH!" Merle would say (if he were here to say it).

Unfortunately, Merle and Pearl's whereabouts were still a mystery to the Gomez family on this last Thursday of November. They had lost the squirrels' trail outside of Jericho. After searching in and around Jerusalem for a couple of weeks with no sign of the squirrels or their squirrelnappers (Ruben and Dr. Simon), Dr. Gomez had felt they had no choice but to return home. Michael, on the other hand, would have preferred to stay.

"You haven't touched your turkey," Mrs. Gomez said.

"I'm not hungry." Michael pouted as he pushed his pea salad around with a fork.

"Look, buddy," Dr. Gomez said. "We couldn't stay in Israel

2

indefinitely without any idea of where the squirrels are."

"It's a small country."

"It's not that small. Plus, you needed to get back to school, and I needed to get back to work."

"And I needed my little Cookies safe at home," Mrs. Gomez added. "Cookies" was Mrs. Gomez's pet name for Michael (which he did not like in the least).

Michael groaned. "Mom! I'm not little, and don't call me Cookies!"

"Are you going to eat your potatoes?" Jane asked.

"Eew. Slimy cat spit fingers!" Michael protested as he pulled his plate away from her.

Jane dipped a finger into her turkey gravy and held it out for Mr. Nemesis. "It's not slimy. It tickles," she said.

"I have contacts who will let me know if they hear any news about the squirrels. If we get a lead, we are only a plane ride away," Dr. Gomez said, placing a reassuring hand on Michael's shoulder.

"But when will that be?!" Michael wondered. "What if we never get any leads?"

"Dr. Simon can't keep them hidden forever," Dr. Gomez replied. "Perhaps he's just waiting it out until he feels the coast is clear . . ."

CHAPTER 2

"I believe the coast is now clear!" Dr. Simon announced over the phone from his safe house in Ein Karem, a small town near Jerusalem. By the way, a "safe house" is what a villain calls his hideout. If you want to know a little inside information on good guys and bad guys, most of the time, villains don't realize they are villains. In his own mind, Dr. Simon was a good guy. He had an ingenious plan that would bring joy to countless children, give attention to the rich history of Israel, AND make him a lot of money. What's so bad about that? What never occurred to him was that kidnapping two talking squirrels, imprisoning them in a birdcage, and concealing their whereabouts from their only friends in the world is a very villainous thing to do.

"So, we are finally ready to move?!" a voice from the other end of the phone responded. The voice belonged to Delilah, the owner of Old Town Nazareth. You may recall that Old Town Nazareth was a theme park re-creation of the first century in the heart of Nazareth, the town where Jesus grew up, about 100 miles north of Ein Karem. Dr. Gomez and Michael had visited the park a couple of months earlier in their search for Merle and Pearl. Delilah continued, "I can't wait to see those squirrels!"

"*SHHHHH!*" Dr. Simon shushed her. "You need to be more discreet. You never know who's listening."

"Forgive me, Doctor. I'll be more careful," Delilah replied. What she failed to realize was that while there were no other people around, she was standing beside the donkey pen of Ham, the talking-donkey nephew of Dusty, who, months before, had revealed to Michael and Dr. Gomez that Merle and Pearl were being smuggled south along the Nativity Trail. "I'll make sure we are ready for the merchandise," Delilah added before hanging up the phone.

As she headed inside, Ham raised

an eyebrow in interest. *"HEE-HAW!"* he bellowed. Which in donkey means, *"Interesting . . ."*

"The coast is clear?" Merle asked from the confines of his and Pearl's large birdcage. Having been imprisoned for the last two months, he had taken up a few hobbies to keep himself from going crazy. At the moment, he happened to be folding an origami frog. "What's it clear of?"

"It's clear of Gomezes!" Dr. Simon snapped. "They've been gone long

8

enough and have most assuredly for-
gotten about you."

"Michael wouldn't forget us!"
Pearl huffed. She had also taken up a
hobby—exercise—and was jogging on
an oversized hamster wheel set up in
the cage. "Merle—would you mind?"
Pearl pointed to the tip of the water
nozzle hanging from the cage. Merle
swung it toward Pearl for a sip.

"We'll see about that!" Dr. Simon laughed as he exited the safe house, leaving Merle and Pearl alone.

Pearl hopped off her hamster wheel, her little squirrel tongue panting away. "I wonder what's become of Dusty?"

"He's probably still trying to find Michael and Dr. Gomez," Merle replied, finishing up a fold on his origami.

"Poor thing has no idea they are back in Tennessee," Pearl said.

"I made you a frog," Merle said as he handed Pearl the paper amphibian.

"Thank you, Merle! I love it!" Pearl answered and set the frog in a tall pile of origami creatures in the corner of the cage.

CHAPTER 3

Hee-Haw!

Dusty brayed, which means in donkey, "I need to find Michael and Dr. Gomez!" The statement was aimed at Adriana, a scraggly, long-necked alpaca.

Hmm...

Adriana hummed,

not because she was thinking about what Dusty said, but because that's just the sound alpacas make. Adriana didn't speak donkey or English—she just liked hanging around Dusty because she thought he was nice. The two had recently been penned up together in what amounted to a donkey retirement community: Donkey Haven Animal Sanctuary. Donkeys are used for all kinds of work in Israel—until they get too old to be useful anymore. Donkey Haven provided a safe place for them to live out the rest of their days,

DON'T WORRY

BE HEE-HAW HAPPY

DONKEY HAVEN
Animal Sanctuary
Getting a kick out of retirement since 1996

and the sanctuary occasionally hosted
other animals, like alpacas.

"I can't stay locked up in here! Let
me out! Let me out!" Dusty complained
loudly (in donkey, of course).

"It's okay, sweetheart." The voice of
a young woman rang out—Rebecca,
a volunteer at Donkey Haven. "You're
safe now. You don't have to worry
about that nasty merry-go-round ever
again." Rebecca approached, carrying
a bucket of carrots. "And how are you
today, Adriana?" she kindly asked as
she rubbed Adriana's fuzzy head.

"Hmm . . ." Adriana said with a
grin.

"Glad to hear it!" Rebecca chirped
and offered them both a carrot.
Adriana gladly accepted, while Dusty
turned up his nose. "That's okay,

13

old-timer. You just let me know when
you want one!" she added with a smile
and headed on her way.

How did a donkey from Galilee end
up at an animal shelter in Judea? If
you recall, two months previously,
Dusty had met Merle and Pearl when
Ruben purchased him from a tour
guide in Nazareth to carry the caged
squirrels to Ein Karem. But as soon
as Merle untied Dusty from the hitch-
ing post outside of Dr. Simon's safe

house, Dusty bolted straight toward
Jerusalem to find Michael and Dr.
Gomez! However, a stray donkey does
not last long on his own in this part
of the world. Almost immediately,
he was spotted and scooped up by a
bricklayer. After a few weeks of heavy
hauling, Dusty managed to wiggle out
of his brick cart straps (much to the
surprise of the bricklayer, who rolled
backward down a hill, screaming atop
his stack of bricks).

Unfortunately, it didn't take much time for a carnival worker to capture the detached donkey and promptly put him to work turning a merry-go-round. There, poor Dusty walked around in circles for another month before being spotted by the kindhearted Rebecca and brought to live in Donkey Haven.

"I'm gonna need your help," Dusty said to Adriana as she polished off her carrot.

"Hmm . . ." Adriana replied.

CHAPTER 4

It's amazing how fast word can travel when a bunch of donkeys get to talking. As Dusty was fond of saying, "Before the internet came along in these parts, there were three major types of communication: telephone, television, and tell-a-donkey." Between the hee-hawing

of all the standard donkeys and the chatter among the handful of English-speaking beasts, it didn't take long for Ham's lead that the squirrels were on the move to find its way to a friend of the Gomezes.

"Hello, Father Phillip!" Dr. Gomez said, excited to spot the caller ID from the good friar on his phone. "Do you have any news?" Father Phillip had become one of Dr. Gomez's trusted contacts in Israel. After having tried to help the squirrels before their capture by Ruben at the Basilica of the Annunciation in Nazareth, the friar had been more than happy to keep his ear to the ground for news of Merle and Pearl.

"Merle and Pearl may be headed back to Nazareth," Father Phillip replied.

Dr. Gomez remembered that Nazareth was where Merle and Pearl had first been brought by Ruben. It made sense. Perhaps Dr. Simon's original plan was back in motion? This could be the news he'd been waiting for. After catching up with the friar for a couple of minutes, Dr. Gomez thanked him and hung up.

Mrs. Gomez had been listening in on the conversation. "You know, you've been traveling to and work-ing in the Holy Land for years, and Jane and I have never been. This might be a good time for a family get-away," she suggested with a grin.

"A family Christmas vacation in the Holy Land?" Dr. Gomez smiled as he dialed his phone.

CHAPTER 5

Yes!

Michael shouted into his phone, raising his peanut butter and jelly sandwich into the air in triumph. Since his mouth was also full of peanut butter and jelly, he launched a shower of crumbs across the lunch table.

Hey!

Justin complained as a stray glob of jelly struck him on the cheek.

"Sorry," Michael said.

"What's up?" Sadie asked, sitting down next to Justin. Now that Thanksgiving break was over, Michael and his best friends had returned to school at Walnut Creek Elementary.

Michael leaned across the table and whispered, "We're going back to find Merle and Pearl!"

"Let's do it!" Sadie squealed.

"Woohoo!" Justin followed.

"What are you nerds so happy about?" Edgar asked as he approached the fifth-grade table, followed by his two minions, Pete and Bruce. "Did you get picked to march in the nerd parade?" Pete and Bruce found Edgar's rapier wit hilarious as usual, laughing like crazy.

"Don't you have potato chips to

steal, Edgar?" Sadie said. "We're having a private conversation."

Sadie's comeback gave Edgar an
idea, and he nabbed a bag of Lay's off
of Pete's tray.

"Hey!" Pete complained as the three
fourth-grade delinquents continued to
their table.

"We can go, right?" Sadie whispered to Michael when the coast was clear. The friends had recently had several conversations about the possibility. Justin had spent the previous summer in Israel with Michael, but Sadie had missed out on the trip. Michael had promised she could go next time.

"Justin and Sadie can come, right?" Michael asked his dad over the phone.

"That's fine with us, but they'll need their parents' permission," Dr. Gomez answered. Michael gave his friends a thumbs-up.

"Yes!" Justin and Sadie exclaimed.

CHAPTER 6

In the dim light of a new moon, Dusty
banged his head against the tightly
spaced split rails of the fence surrounding Donkey Haven. *If only I can squeeze
my head through and reach the latch on
the other side of the gate*, he thought.
If you have ever seen a donkey on a
farm or in a petting zoo (and have pet-
ted their head), you know how difficult this would be. Donkeys' heads are
huge.

When you are a donkey working
for a Holy Land tour operator, hauling bricks, or driving a merry-go-
round, you spend quite a bit of time,
if not all of the time, tied up. This

makes escaping very difficult. In fact, if Rebecca had not noticed poor old Dusty being forced to walk in endless circles, he'd probably still be walking in endless circles. At the retirement community, Dusty's fortunes had improved considerably. He could roam freely, wherever he wanted—as long as he stayed inside the pen. However, the fact remained that he still had a job to do: find Michael and Dr. Gomez, or at least get word back to Merle and Pearl that he couldn't find them. He needed to complete his mission, which meant that he needed to escape.

After trying out a variety of angles and levels of force to squeeze his head through the rails, Dusty noticed something out of the corner of his eye:

Adriana effortlessly sticking her head
in and out of the rails, mimicking him.

"Hmm . . ." Adriana hummed,
noticing Dusty's glare.

Dusty brightened. Adriana could be
his ticket out of here! Since this pen
was designed for donkeys, not alpacas,
perhaps she could do what he could
not.

"Do you think you can reach the latch?!" Dusty whispered in donkey.

"Hmm . . ." Adriana answered, blankly.

"Right. You can't understand me," Dusty remembered. When people don't speak the same language, sometimes the best way to communicate is by pointing and smiling. It's the same for animals. After several long minutes of head motions and forced smiles, Dusty was finally able to get his idea across to Adriana. When she at last understood what he wanted, Adriana had no problem at all sticking her small fluffy head and long flexible neck out of the pen and unlatching the gate with her muscular alpaca lips.

"There! That wasn't so hard, was it?" Dusty whispered. "Thanks!"

"Hmm . . ." Adriana replied as the gate swung open. The two furry fugitives escaped into the darkness.

CHAPTER 7

"Well, what do you think?" Merle called out as Pearl sprinted along on the hamster wheel.

"Think about what?" Pearl huffed as she turned her head in the direction of Merle's voice. Instead of sporting his typical brownish fur, Merle appeared to have gone completely white. "*AHHH!*" Pearl yelled.

"Pretty good, huh?!" Merle boasted as he stepped up alongside his pale impostor. "I origamied myself!" Sure enough, Merle had convincingly re-created himself in paper: a bona fide origami Merle Squirrel.

"Wow, Merle, that's terrifying, but

impressive." Pearl hopped off the wheel.
"I'm glad you're using your time in
squirrel prison constructively."

"I sense a little sarcasm in your
tone," Merle replied.

"You should really try exercising.
I've never felt better in my whole life:
I feel 2,000 years younger," Pearl
added, doing toe touches.

Merle looked around the room to check for listening ears. There were no signs of Ruben or Dr. Simon. "I've got a plan," he whispered.

"A plan for what?" Pearl whispered back.

"A plan for escape," Merle replied in an even lower whisper.

"What?" Pearl asked. "Whisper a little louder."

"An escape plan," Merle repeated, more audibly.

"What is it?" Pearl peered around the room herself.

"I'll make a paper you, too. We leave our origami doppelgängers in our beds—pull the covers up, like we're sleeping. Ruben won't discover it's not actually us for a long time—and by the time he does, we'll be long gone!" he proclaimed proudly.

Pearl thought Merle's plan sounded promising, nodding along as it unfolded. "I have a question, though," she said. "How are we supposed to get out of the cage?"

Merle stared back with an expression a lot like his lifeless origami self. "Um . . . I guess I haven't figured that part out yet."

"It's kind of the most important part?" Pearl said as she continued with her toe touches.

"One thing at a time," Merle replied, grabbing his paper Merle and heading back to his folding corner.

CHAPTER 8

It took quite a bit of desperate convinc-
ing, pleading, and promising, along
with a fair amount of pouting and out-
right begging from Justin and Sadie for
their parents to allow them
to spend Christmas with
the Gomezes in Israel.
Fortunately, because
only a couple of weeks

of school remained before Christmas vacation, Michael and his two best friends were able to get a sign-off from Mr. P. (the principal at Walnut Creek Elementary School) for an educational trip—as long as they finished all their assignments online and on time.

"We'll be back before New Year's!" Michael proclaimed confidently as their plane touched down in Haifa.

"You think we can find Merle and Pearl before then?" Justin asked a little less confidently, as they picked up their luggage from baggage claim.

"It could take longer than that," Sadie said with a hopeful smile. Since she had missed out on spending the previous summer at the Dead Sea with Michael and Justin, she wouldn't mind a longer stay.

"I did promise your parents we'd have you back before the start of school," Mrs. Gomez cautioned as they exited immigration and customs.

A voice rang out in greeting. "How are my favorite squirrel-loving friends?"

"Father Phillip!" Michael yelled and ran to give the friar a hug. "What are you doing here?"

"I live here!" Father Phillip replied with a smile. "Besides, this is a big group. You all won't fit into a rental car. This is a job for a church van!"

"I can't thank you

enough for keeping an ear out for the
squirrels, Father." Dr. Gomez beamed
as he shook the friar's hand. "Where
to first?"

"I think Old Town Nazareth is the
best place to start."

"What's Old Town Nazareth?" Justin
asked Michael.

"It's a theme park," Michael replied.

"The best trip ever!" Sadie squealed.

CHAPTER 9

"I wasn't thinking you'd be coming with me," Dusty said to Adriana as the two slunk quietly through a grove of trees on the outskirts of Jerusalem. He had grown used to talking to her, even though he knew full well she couldn't understand him. "I don't want you to get into trouble."

"Hmm . . ." Adriana said, as always.

Two unattended animals sneaking through the suburbs might be easier to spot than just one, but Dusty was nonetheless happy to have the company. Four hard donkey hooves and eight alpaca toes clomping on pavement could make a huge racket, so they were careful to tiptoe along as silently as possible on unpaved grassy areas, which included parks, forests, and a few lawns.

Because it had been months since he had first started his search, Dusty had long given up hope of trying to find Michael and Dr. Gomez. But he knew exactly where Merle and Pearl were— or at least where they had been the last time he saw them. And after a few hours of creeping through the darkness, they arrived at their destination.

"Merle! What's that?!" Pearl whispered from her bed of wood chips in their cozy squirrel slammer.

"Mmmmm," Merle replied—his typical response to a question while sleeping.

"I think someone's outside," Pearl whispered. No sooner had the words left her lips than the front door exploded open with a loud *BANG*, splinters and dust flying!

WAAAAAA!

Merle screamed, popping straight up into the air, then down into Pearl's arms.

"*AHHHHH!*" Pearl added—a scream which would have gone on longer had she not had to catch Merle. Through the settling cloud of dirt and splinters, the squirrels could make out the backside of a donkey. "Dusty?" Pearl gasped.

Dusty turned his head into the room and smiled. "I hoped you'd still be here!"

with all the noise Dusty had made
kicking the door down, it would not
be long before Ruben arrived.

"How do I do that?!" Dusty asked,
desperately.

Before Merle or Pearl could answer,
Adriana grabbed a splinter of wood
from the shattered door in her lips and
inserted the sharp end into the lock.

CHAPTER 10

Dusty rushed to Merle and Pearl and grabbed the top of the cage with his teeth, attempting to lift it off the table. However, when he jerked his head to the side to make a run for the door, the cage stayed put and nearly took a couple of the donkey's teeth with it. "Errg!" Dusty grunted.

"It's attached to the table!" Merle warned, a little too late. Angry at the squirrels' previous escape attempt, Ruben was taking no chances and had screwed the cage down tight.

"You're gonna have to break us out!" Pearl shouted. "And hurry! Before we get caught!" Pearl felt for sure that

With a couple of skillful twists and wiggles, she picked the lock open.

"Who is this?!" Pearl asked, impressed, as she hopped out of the cage.

"A-Adriana," Dusty replied, stunned. "How did you do that?!" he asked the alpaca.

"Hmm . . ." she replied, spitting out the splinter.

45

"Merle! Let's go!" Pearl called back to her husband, who was gathering up an armload of origami.

"Coming!" Merle answered as he exited, his arms overflowing with his folded treasures.

Just then, Ruben appeared in the doorway. "You again!" he shouted, his eyes narrowing on Dusty.

"*HEE-HAW!*" Dusty bellowed, which in English means, "Follow me!," and

rushed toward the door, straight toward Ruben, who, not interested in being run over by a donkey, dove out of the way. Adriana, Pearl, and Merle followed Dusty's charge outside.

"Wait up!" Merle shouted from behind his paper payload.

"Get rid of those things!" Pearl called back. "They're slowing you down!" She was partly right—Merle would have been able to run a little faster unencumbered by his cargo, but because Pearl had chosen to exercise during their time in captivity rather than sit around and fold paper, she was also now a much faster runner.

Ruben exited the safe house in hot pursuit of the fleeing animals, and it did not take him long to catch up to the lumbering Merle.

"*AHHH!*" Merle yelled and deployed the origami of himself in a futile attempt to throw Ruben off.

Other than pausing briefly for a confused glance, Ruben continued his pursuit, diving forward and grabbing on to the out-of-shape squirrel! "Gotcha!" he called out.

"Merle!!!" Pearl shouted out desperately as she looked back at her captured husband.

CHAPTER 11

Had Dusty, Adriana, and Pearl been able to sneak away into the surrounding hills, they might have been able to avoid recapture. However, since they remained outside the grounds of Dr. Simon's safe house plotting Merle's rescue, it didn't take long for a passing motorist to notice a donkey and an alpaca crouched behind a tree.

"What do we have here?" the truck driver wondered as his headlights revealed the poorly concealed trio. "Christmas has come early!" he laughed.

"Not again," Dusty sighed, recalling how he had been captured by a bricklayer soon after escaping from the safe house. "Run!" he bellowed, bolting to the right. Pearl, with an anguished look back at Merle's prison, took off running in the opposite direction.

However, Adriana remained completely still. If you've ever heard of the term "frozen like an alpaca in the head-lights" (which you probably haven't, because it usually just applies to deer), you would know that she was blinded by the bright lights and was basically hypnotized.

Hmm...

she hummed lightly as a smile slowly spread across her alpaca lips. Before Dusty could circle back to nudge her out of the bright beams, a lasso sailed out of the darkness and flopped over her head, tightening around her neck like a leash.

51

"A little fuzzy camel," the driver said as he walked into the light holding the other end of the rope. "This'll be a first!"

"*Hee-Haw!*" Dusty protested.

"We've got plenty of donkeys—you can run along," the driver answered.

Dusty stood his ground, having no intention of leaving his friend. Pearl scurried up alongside Dusty.

"Ha!" The driver laughed. "I guess everybody wants to be a star. Why not? You both can come too."

"*URRRRRG!*" a very tall and very grumpy camel grunted, not at all happy to have three new passengers crammed into the cargo hold. Among the other occupants were a few sheep, goats, and chickens, along with one

ox, a couple of cows, and a non-English-speaking donkey. The camel's grumble set off a chain reaction of complaints from the other animals.

"Quiet down—we don't have far to go!" the truck driver bellowed as he slammed the trailer gate shut.

"You two look like you could be related," Pearl noted, glancing between Adriana and the camel.

"Hmm . . ." Adriana cluelessly hummed.

"There is a resemblance," Dusty confirmed.

Fun fact: Alpacas and camels are actually related—they are both members of the biological family Camelidae and share many similar features (except for the alpaca's lack of height and humps).

The truck lurched forward and continued on with its new occupants.

CHAPTER 12

SLAM!

The cage door of squirrel prison shut fast, and Ruben refastened the lock. "How did you open this?!" he demanded. "I'm the only one with a key!"

"Evidently, alpacas are master lock pickers," Merle responded, still out of breath from his out-of-shape sprint. "Who knew?!"

"All I know is that Dr. Simon can't find out that Pearl escaped."

"Technically, I escaped too . . ."

"You don't count—I got you back."

"It counted for me," Merle argued.

"It's been months since I felt the wind in my tail. Tell you what I'll do for you," he offered, grabbing a fresh piece of paper. "I'll make a substitute Pearl, and Dr. Simon will never know."

Ruben grunted grumpily and headed out the doorless doorway to try to find Pearl.

"You'll never find her!" Merle called after him, defiantly, savoring the sound of his words. After a few moments of satisfaction, Merle glanced over to the hamster wheel and set down the paper. "I need to get back into shape," he resolved.

CHAPTER 13

"I recognize this place," Dusty whispered to Pearl as the animals disembarked from the truck after a short 30-minute drive. Having been a Holy Land tour donkey for most of his life, he was very familiar with popular tourist destinations.

"Where did you find an alpaca?" a woman with a clipboard asked the truck driver as Adriana waddled down the ramp.

"What are you talking about? It's a little fuzzy camel! I'll give you a good deal on her and even throw in an extra donkey and squirrel!" the truck driver replied before launching into a negotiation with the woman for his bonus cargo.

"Where are we?" Pearl whispered as they stepped inside a stable set up just outside of a large, ancient-looking church.

"The Church of the Nativity! In Bethlehem!" Dusty replied.

Pearl looked around excitedly. "The town where Jesus was born?"

"Exactly! I've heard the story many times and know it by heart if you'd like to hear," Dusty offered.

Pearl nodded. "Merle and I didn't get to see him until he was older. I'd love to hear the story of his birth!"

Alone with the animals inside the stable and out of earshot of humans, Dusty began. "At that time—you know, your time, about 2,000 years ago—the Roman emperor, Augustus, decreed that a census should be taken throughout the Roman Empire."

"Oooh! I remember him!" Pearl said. "He was never very popular in Galilee."

"Yeah, I wouldn't think so," Dusty replied, then continued, "These days, every family just fills out a census form and sends it back in the mail. But in those days, everyone needed to travel to their hometowns to be counted. So, even though Joseph and Mary were living way up north in the town of

Nazareth, and even though Mary was super pregnant, they needed to travel to Bethlehem—the town where Joseph's ancestors were from, including King David."

"The same way we traveled with you on the Nativity Trail!" Pearl remembered.

"Yep! It took at least a couple of weeks. So, they roll into town, and Mary is like,

Uh-oh. Here comes the baby!

But since so many people were on the
road traveling, finding a proper place
to have a baby was really difficult.
This is way before hospitals, motels, or
Airbnb."

"So, they found a stable?" Pearl
asked, looking around at the other animals in the barnlike display where they
were gathered.

"Exactly!" Dusty replied. "And Mary gave birth to Jesus, wrapped the baby in strips of cloth, and laid him in a manger, which is a basin used to hold food for animals."

Pearl now realized why the driver had taken them, along with the rest of the animals, to Bethlehem: to re-create the scene of Jesus' birth. She so wished Merle could be here to see this.

"Meanwhile, just outside of town," Dusty continued, "an angel of the Lord appeared to a group of shepherds. They were terrified, but the angel calmed them down and said, 'Don't be afraid! I bring you good news that will bring great joy to all people. The Savior— yes, the Messiah, the Lord—has been born today in Bethlehem, the city of David! And you will recognize him by this sign: You will find a baby wrapped snugly in strips of cloth, lying in a manger.'"

"God sent Jesus to rescue his people—his children," Pearl realized.

"And all of heaven rejoiced." Dusty smiled. "The angel was joined by a vast host of others—the armies of heaven— praising God and saying, 'Glory to God in highest heaven, and peace on earth to those with whom God is pleased.' When the angels returned to heaven, the shepherds ran here to Bethlehem. They arrived to find Joseph, Mary, and the baby lying in a manger, just like the angels had said."

Pearl smiled as she looked around at the ancient City of David and toward the church built on the site where Jesus was born, amazed and thankful that God would send a Savior.

CHAPTER 14

OLD TOWN NAZARETH
Theme Park

"Welcome to Old Town Nazareth!" the chipper guide announced as she began the tour. The last time Michael and Dr. Gomez had visited the popular tourist site, they were placed with a group of six strangers. This time, however, since there were seven people traveling in the Gomez group, including Father Phillip, they got their very own guide, whom Michael recognized.

"Hi, Hannah!" Michael called out and was met with a friendly smile and wave from Hannah, who was not surprised to be named given that her badge read, *Hi, my name is Hannah.*

"Hi there! What's your name?" she asked with a chirp.

"I was here before—remember me?" Michael beamed.

"Umm . . ." She stumbled, trying to recall. The truth is tour guides can run across hundreds of people in a day, and thousands over the course of a couple of months.

"I asked you about the animals," Michael clarified. This was also no help, since most kids who came through on tours asked about the animals.

Dr. Gomez jumped in. "My son

couldn't stop asking about the animals. Would it be possible to see them?"

"Oh yes," Hannah answered. "We'll pass by the sheep, goats, and donkey pens in a little bit."

"Would it be okay to see them first?" Michael offered. "I really like the animals. I know where they are."

This request threw Hannah off. "Well, that's not really how we . . ."

"Tell you what," Dr. Gomez offered. "What if you continue on with the tour while my son and I run over to check out the animals, and we'll catch back up

with you? He's really been looking forward to seeing them again."

Hannah, confused by what could be so fascinating about a few goats and a donkey, nonetheless agreed to the request. However, when Michael and Dr. Gomez headed out to the animal pen, they were promptly followed by Justin and Sadie, leaving just Mrs. Gomez, Father Phillip, and Jane with the puzzled guide. "Um . . . who wants to see how they made clothes in the first century?" Hannah asked.

"Me!" Jane squealed.

"I haven't heard anything more about squirrels," Ham whispered from inside the donkey pen. "But my uncle Dusty is stirring things up down in Jerusalem."

"What do you mean?" Michael asked, glancing over his shoulder to make sure no one was watching or listening. Justin and Sadie stood by with their mouths agape, in shock to hear a donkey whispering.

"Word on the street is that he escaped from a place called Donkey Haven, along with an alpaca," Ham said.

"Alpaca?" Dr. Gomez raised a brow, knowing that alpacas were a South American animal and not at all common in this part of the world. "That's odd."

"I'm just telling you what I heard. But there's more," Ham continued, shifting his eyes from side to side. "It may be a coincidence, but it's also going around that the Church of the Nativity in Bethlehem is featuring its first-ever live alpaca in the Christmas manger display."

"Hmm . . ." Dr. Gomez noted with interest.

Just then, a voice called out from the

distance. "Can I help you?" Dr. Gomez and the kids turned to see a woman approaching—Delilah, the park owner. "Did you lose your tour group?" she asked, trying to come off as friendly, but only succeeding in sounding suspicious.

"We love the animals," Michael said nervously.

"Thank you," the park manager replied skeptically. "Americans?" she asked, recognizing the accent. The kids and Dr. Gomez nodded their heads as Ham dipped his head down to grab a mouthful of hay.

"Yes, ma'am," Michael replied.

"Hmm . . ." Delilah continued, looking them up and down. "Allow me to reunite you with your tour group." She motioned for them to follow her, giving

Ham the stink eye as the donkey
sheepishly munched on his hay.

CHAPTER 15

"Are you sure you don't mind us borrowing the van?" Dr. Gomez asked Father Phillip as they pulled up to the Basilica of the Annunciation.

Father Phillip opened the passenger-side door and stepped out. "Absolutely not!" he said. "You'll need it more than me. My work this time of year is all at the church. I wish I could join you, but Christmas is our busy season! Of course, I'll keep my ear to the ground up here in the north." Dr. Gomez and the kids promised to keep Father Phillip posted on their search before exchanging Merry Christmas greetings and heading on their way.

The route from Nazareth to Bethlehem was a familiar one for Dr. Gomez and Michael, who had traveled the same way months before in their search for Dusty and the squirrels. However, since they didn't have to search every nook and cranny of the countryside along the way, the drive was going much faster this time.

"If we can find that alpaca, we can hopefully locate Dusty," Dr. Gomez explained to Mrs. Gomez as they zoomed down Highway 90 along the Jordan River.

"And if we can find Dusty, there's a good chance he'll know where to find Merle and Pearl, if they're not with him already," Michael speculated from the second row of the van next to Justin.

Sadie and Jane in her car seat occupied the third row.

"What's the Church of the Nativity, Dr. Gomez?" Justin asked.

"I can tell you that," Sadie offered from the back row before Dr. Gomez had a chance to respond. She had a large travel book of Israel open on her lap. "Originally built by Constantine in AD 333, and later rebuilt by Justinian in the sixth century, the church sits on what is considered to be the birthplace of Jesus. It's one of the

oldest churches in the world still in use today."

"You brought an encyclopedia?" Michael remarked with surprise.

"For one, it's not an encyclopedia, and two, did you expect me to come not prepared?" Sadie responded. "The annual lighting of the Christmas tree in Bethlehem near the church is accompanied by a live crèche featuring actors, human and animal alike, re-creating the Nativity at the time of Jesus' birth."

"That sounds lovely!" Mrs. Gomez said.

"I sure hope Ham was right," Michael added.

CHAPTER 16

After Pearl's escape from the safe house in Ein Karem, Ruben spent the next few days searching around Jerusalem for his fugitives. Eventually, he stumbled upon a flyer announcing the first-ever Nativity alpaca in Bethlehem. The flyer displayed a clear picture of Adriana lying by a manger, dressed to look like a camel (including a miniature hump). Behind her stood Dusty, and above the whole scene hung Pearl from a string in a pair of angel wings.

"Aha!" Ruben exclaimed and headed toward Bethlehem.

"I can't feel my legs," Pearl whispered down to Dusty. She loved her little cherub costume, but being suspended in a tiny squirrel harness for hours on end was not good for her circulation.

"Did you say something?" the teenage boy dressed up like Joseph said to dressed-up Mary.

"No. We're not supposed to talk," Mary said. "Silent night, remember?"

"Shhhhh," Dusty cautioned Pearl.

"See? Even the donkey knows that," Mary continued.

"Donkeys can't shush," Joseph whispered.

"Shhhhh," Mary shushed.

Outside of the Nativity, the crowd milled by, enjoying the crisp evening air and holiday sights. Despite losing sensation in her legs, Pearl loved to

look out at the children passing with
big smiles on their faces, pointing to
the squirrel angel and the mini camel.
Dusty had told her that this could last
a couple of weeks, so when she wasn't
taking in the admiration of the masses,
she was thinking about how to escape
and get back to Merle.

Pearl? a voice called out
from the crowd. Pearl looked toward
the sound of the voice and could not

believe her eyes. She blinked a few times to make sure she was not seeing things: it was Michael, flanked by Justin and Sadie, headed through the crowd toward her! Knowing that it wouldn't be a good idea to call back with Joseph, Mary, and the shepherds standing around, Pearl smiled broadly and vigorously waved her numb paws.

However, her look of joy soon turned to horror when she spotted Ruben right behind Michael! He too was now making a beeline through the crowd toward her! Michael and Ruben had found her at the same time! Ruben didn't even notice Michael, Justin, and Sadie as he pushed past them, barreling his way toward Pearl.

"*SQUEAK, SQUEAK!*" Pearl chattered in squirrel to Dusty while motioning to the approaching Ruben. Dusty didn't understand squirrel, but her tone clearly indicated danger. He turned his head and immediately spotted Ruben, but before Dusty could intercept him, Ruben broke past the railings of the Nativity and lunged toward Pearl.

"Hey!" Joseph shouted.

"Shhhhh!" Mary shushed.

Pearl swung herself back and forth— the only thing she could do to avoid being a sitting duck. As Ruben reached out to grab Pearl, Dusty rushed at Ruben's legs, knocking him forward so his hand bumped into Pearl and pushed her up toward the ceiling.

"*SQUEAK!*" Pearl yelled, swinging much higher and faster as Ruben fell to the straw-covered ground with a thud. Adriana saw

her chance to help, and as Pearl swung
past, she stuck her long neck up and
bit into Pearl's string.

Pearl went flying out of the Nativity
with a louder *"SQUEAK!"*

"*SHHHHH!!!*" Mary shushed in
exasperation.

CHAPTER 17

"Get back here!" Ruben called, standing up and resuming his pursuit. Dusty and Adriana followed after him through the broken railings.

"*AHHH!*" The crowd encircling the front of the Nativity gasped and pushed back at the sight of a charging donkey and miniature camel-alpaca. This allowed Michael, Justin, and Sadie a clear path to also give chase.

Little angel Pearl with her wings flapping in the breeze and a length of string trailing behind her darted into the courtyard of the church, her claws tapping against the tiled ground. She frantically looked left and right for some path of escape, but only high walls surrounded her—the ancient stone walls of the church to her right and a brick fence to the left. A heavy wooden door, the entrance to the church, lay in front of her—closed. She stopped fast, her paws skidding on the hard tile. She turned to see Ruben drawing closer.

"You're cornered, Pearl! I've got you now!" Ruben called out with a huff. Pearl looked around in desperation for any possible escape route and spotted a high windowsill in the side of the church, about 10 feet off the ground. If you've ever seen a really, really old stone building like a castle, you'll know that the lime mortar that binds the stones together can wear away over time and leave gaps between the stones. If you happen to have really small feet (or really small paws with claws on them), there is enough space between the stones to climb! Pearl sprinted toward the wall and jumped up toward one of those gaps, catching it with her front paws, then scampered up the wall toward the windowsill. She looked over her shoulder as she climbed to see Ruben racing toward the wall along with Dusty, Adriana, Michael, Justin, and Sadie not too far behind.

"Ha ha!" Pearl called out in relief upon reaching the sill. She was too high up for Ruben to reach her, and his feet were too big to climb up the wall after her.

So why was he smiling?

THE STRING! Pearl realized in horror

that the string attached to her was dangling four feet off the ground. She reached out to pull up the strand right as Ruben reached for the bottom of it to pull her down! But just as his fingers were closing around the thread, *THUMP!* A fake mini camel hump collided with his head, engulfing it fully in hollow acrylic.

"Jump, Pearl!" Michael called out as Ruben wriggled along the ground, trying to remove his unwelcome helmet, a task made difficult by its extremely tight fit. Pearl wasted no time in leaping down onto Adriana's soft, fluffy, hump-less back, and the friends escaped into the crowd.

CHAPTER 18

"Where were you?!" Dr. Gomez
demanded as Michael dashed into the
square outside of the church. Moments
earlier, the family had barely parked
the van before Jane had become dis-
tracted by the enormous Christmas
tree and had run toward it. As Dr.
and Mrs. Gomez had chased after her,
Michael, Justin, and Sadie had spotted
the Nativity and headed in the opposite direction.

"We were rescuing Pearl just in time."
Michael beamed proudly. Shoving
through the crowd behind him were
Justin, Sadie, Dusty, and an angelic
Pearl riding on an alpaca.

"What in the world?!" Mrs. Gomez gasped.

"Pearl!" Jane chirped with glee.

"That was easy," Dr. Gomez commented.

"Not really," Sadie said. "Ruben's right behind us!"

"But where's Merle?" Dr. Gomez asked.

"Ein Karem," Dusty said.

"*AHHH!*" Mrs. Gomez screamed, shocked by the talking donkey. "I'm sorry," she apologized, recovering. "I should have gotten used to this by now."

"Let's get to the hotel and figure out our next step," Dr. Gomez added.

After determining they would need to remove at least one row of seats from the van to fit a donkey and an alpaca, Dr. Gomez and Michael walked Dusty and Adriana back to the hotel, which was only a couple of blocks away, while Mrs. Gomez drove the others. That was the easy part—getting *in* the hotel with a donkey and an alpaca was another story.

It was Justin who figured out a solution. "Just stay still," he whispered as the kids pushed Dusty and Adriana across the lobby on a luggage cart. "Everyone will think you are giant stuffed animals." Pearl heeded the same advice, remaining motionless as Jane carried her stuffed angel squirrel to the elevators.

"We really like animals," Michael noted to the shocked onlookers.

Once inside their suite, Pearl and Dusty filled everyone in on the events of the past couple of months, their escape from the safe house, and Merle's recapture.

"We need to get to Merle right away," Pearl urged.

"I think you're right," Dr. Gomez added. "If Ruben knows that we know where he is, he's sure to move Merle to another location."

The family decided that Mrs. Gomez and Jane would remain in the hotel with Dusty and Adriana, while Dr. Gomez, Michael, Pearl, Justin, and Sadie would head out to Ein Karem.

CHAPTER 19

MERLE!

Pearl (no longer dressed like an angel) cried as the rescue party poured through the doorless entry of Dr. Simon's safe house. But the hatch to their bolted-down squirrel prison lay open with no Merle in sight.

"You said Ruben brought him back in here?" Sadie asked.

"That's right," Pearl lamented. "We were watching from the woods and planning our rescue when we were rounded up for the Nativity."

"Ruben must have just beat us here," Justin said.

"Hey, guys—check this out." Michael was standing on the threshold of an adjacent room. The others followed him into what could best be described as a model room. Not like a room in a model home that's professionally decorated, but a room where models are displayed—in this case, an enormous scale replica of a small town.

"What is this?" Justin asked.

"It looks like a theme park." Sadie pointed at the merry-go-round in the center of the model and the roller coaster lining one end of it.

"It's a zoo," Pearl said, spotting a group of miniature animal pens.

Michael frowned. "Then this is one huge zoo."

"'The most extraordinary petting zoo the world has ever known,' according to Dr. Simon," Pearl confirmed.

Dr. Gomez was looking at the art on the walls. "Balaam's donkey . . . the serpent . . ." He turned to the kids and Pearl. "Talking animals from the Bible?"

"Those are the only ones the Bible mentions," Pearl clarified, having heard the speech from Dr. Simon previously.

"Zephaniah's Cockatoo . . . Perch of Galilee . . ." Dr. Gomez noted as he walked along the wall of paintings.

"That's why he's after you and Merle," Michael deduced.

Sadie crossed her arms. "To be on display at the world's largest petting zoo?" she asked, indignant. She didn't like the idea of the squirrels being taken advantage of in that way.

"Not just on display," Pearl said, "but on display and available for petting."

"Oh no," Michael realized. "Merle's not really the touchy-feely type."

"That's exactly what he said," Pearl remembered.

"This is enormous—much bigger than Old Town Nazareth. Dr. Simon must have been planning this for years," Dr. Gomez said, now examining the model in the middle of the room.

"What are we going to do about Merle?" Michael worried.

CHAPTER 20

"It smells like a manger in here,"
Justin noted as the failed rescue party
returned to the hotel suite.

"You mean a stable," Sadie cor-
rected. "A manger is a feeding trough
for animals. A stable is where animals
live."

"This is one nice stable!" Dusty commented, lying back on the bed, hooves
kicked up and watching TV. Jane
had her luggage opened already and
was busy dressing up Adriana in her
clothes and her mom's makeup.

"Hmm . . ." Adriana hummed,
happy to be doted on.

"It's a little cramped in here, but it's

exciting to be celebrating Christmas in Bethlehem," Mrs. Gomez said. Sadie and Justin agreed, nodding their heads as they hopped up next to Dusty.

"And a great season for a rescue mission," Dusty added, recalling the story of Jesus in the manger.

"We'll start our search for Merle first thing in the morning," Dr. Gomez said with a nod, noting Michael and Pearl's concerned looks.

Meanwhile, on a dark Highway 1 between Jerusalem and Jericho, Merle sat

locked in the trunk of Ruben's car as it
zoomed east toward the Dead Sea—the
last place on earth he wanted to be!

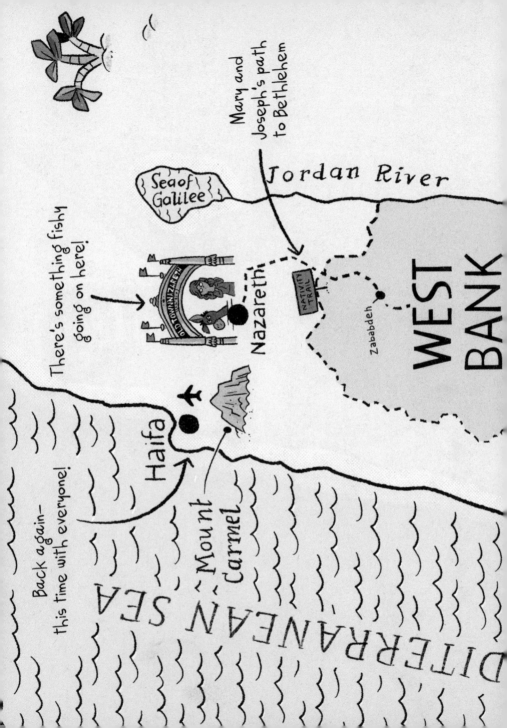

Tel Aviv
Dr. Simon's nefarious plans!
SAFE HOUSE
DONKEY HAVEN
Animal Sanctuary
Dusty makes a break for it!
Ein Karem
Jerusalem
Bethlehem
Dead Sea
There's no place Merle would rather NOT be!
I can't feel my legs!

MICHAEL GOMEZ is an adventurous and active 10-year-old boy. He is kindhearted but often acts before he thinks. He's friendly and talkative and blissfully unaware that most of his classmates think he's a bit geeky. Michael is super excited to be in fifth grade, which, in his mind, makes him "grade school royalty!"

MERLE SQUIRREL may be thousands of years old, but he never really grew up. He has endless enthusiasm for anything new and interesting—especially this strange modern world he finds himself in. He marvels at the self-refilling bowl of fresh drinking water (otherwise known as a toilet) and supplements his regular diet of tree nuts with what he believes might be the world's most perfect food: chicken nuggets. He's old enough to know better, but he often finds it hard to do better. Good thing he's got his wife, Pearl, to help him make wise choices.

PEARL SQUIRREL is wise beyond her many, many, many years, with enough common sense for both her and Merle. When Michael's in a bind, she loves to share a lesson or bit of wisdom from Bible events she witnessed in her youth. Pearl's biggest quirk is that she is a nut hoarder. Having come from a world where food is scarce, her instinct is to grab whatever she can. The abundance and variety of nuts in present-day Tennessee can lead to distraction and storage issues.

JUSTIN KESSLER is Michael's best friend.
Justin is quieter and has better judgment than
Michael, and he is super smart. He's a rule
follower and is obsessed with being on time.
He'll usually give in to what Michael wants
to do after warning him of the likely conse-
quences.

SADIE HENDERSON is Michael and Justin's other best friend. She enjoys video games and bowling just as much as cheerleading and pajama parties. She gets mad respect from her classmates as the only kid at Walnut Creek Elementary who's not afraid of school bully Edgar. Though Sadie's in a different homeroom than her two best friends, the three always sit together at lunch and hang out after class.

DR. GOMEZ, a professor of anthropology, is not thrilled when he finds out that his son, Michael, smuggled two ancient squirrels home from their summer trip to the Dead Sea, but he ends up seeing great value in having them around as original sources for his research. Dad loves his son's adventurous spirit but wishes Michael would look (or at least peek) before he leaps.

MRS. GOMEZ teaches part-time at her daughter's preschool and is a full-time mom to Michael and Jane. She feels sorry for the fish-out-of-water squirrels and looks for ways to help them feel at home, including constructing and decorating an over-the-top hamster mansion for Merle and Pearl in Michael's room. She also can't help but call Michael by her favorite (and his least favorite) nickname, Cookies.

MR. NEMESIS is the Gomez family cat who becomes Merle and Pearl's true nemesis. Jealous of the time and attention given to the squirrels by his family, Mr. Nemesis is continuously coming up with brilliant and creative ways to get rid of them. He hides his ability to talk from the family, but not the squirrels.

JANE GOMEZ is Michael's little sister. She's super adorable but delights in getting her brother busted so she can be known as the "good child." She thinks Merle and Pearl are the cutest things she has ever seen in her whole life (next to Mr. Nemesis) and is fond of dressing them up in her doll clothes.

RUBEN, previously known only as "the man in the suit and sunglasses," has been on the squirrels' tails ever since Michael discovered them at the Dead Sea. Ruben is determined to capture and deliver the refugee rodents to his boss in Israel. He's clever and inventive, but then again, so are the squirrels! Ruben struggles to stay one step ahead of Merle and Pearl.

DR. SIMON is the director of the Jerusalem Antiquities Museum and Ruben's boss. The mastermind behind the creation of the world's first and largest talking-animal petting zoo, he'll stop at nothing to make sure Merle and Pearl headline the grand opening of his theme park alongside a bevy of other babbling biblical beasts.

FATHER PHILLIP is a kind and helpful friar who first encounters Merle and Pearl at the Basilica of the Annunciation in Nazareth. He becomes a trusted local ally of Dr. Gomez and Michael, keeping an ear to the ground for the whereabouts of the squirrels as they are smuggled about Israel.

ADRIANA hails from South America (like all alpacas), so how did she end up in Israel? No one knows for sure, but what is certain is that Adriana is the best friend a donkey could ask for and president of the Dusty Fan Club. She can't speak, but she can pick locks with her lips and has a knack for being in the right place at the right time.

DUSTY is a retired Holy Land tour donkey, purchased by Ruben for agorot on the shekel (pennies on the dollar) to transport Merle and Pearl from Galilee to Judea. The squirrels soon discover that Dusty can also speak human and is a direct descendant of Balaam's donkey of biblical fame.

DR. GOMEZ'S
Historical Handbook

So now you've heard of the Dead Sea Squirrels, but what about the
DEAD SEA *SCROLLS*?

Way back in 1946, just after the end of World War II, in a cave along the banks of the Dead Sea, a 15-year-old boy came across some jars containing ancient scrolls while looking after his goats. When scholars and archaeologists found out about his discovery, the hunt for more scrolls was on! Over the next 10 years, many more scrolls and pieces of scrolls were found in 11 different caves.

121

There are different theories about exactly who wrote on the scrolls and hid them in the caves. One of the most popular ideas is that they belonged to a group of Jewish priests called Essenes, who lived in the desert because they had been thrown out of Jerusalem. One thing is for sure—the scrolls are very, very old! They were placed in the caves between the years 300 BC and AD 100!

Forty percent of the words on the scrolls come from the Bible. Parts of every Old Testament book except for the book of Esther have been discovered.

Of the remaining 60 percent, half are religious texts not found in the Bible, and half are historical records about the way people lived 2,000 years ago.

The discovery of the Dead Sea Scrolls is one of the most important archaeological finds in history!

About the Author

As co-creator of VeggieTales, co-founder of Big Idea Entertainment, and the voice of the beloved Larry the Cucumber, **MIKE NAWROCKI** has been dedicated to helping parents pass on biblical values to their kids through storytelling for over two decades. Mike currently serves as assistant professor of film and animation at Lipscomb University in Nashville, Tennessee, and makes his home in nearby Franklin with his wife, Lisa, and their two children. The Dead Sea Squirrels is Mike's first children's book series.

Find out what happens next in
Risky River Rescue!

Don't go nuts waiting to
find out what happens to

Get the next book today!

Watch out for more adventures with
Merle, Pearl, and all their friends!

SADDLE UP AND JOIN WINNIE AND HER FAMILY AT THE WILLIS WYOMING RANCH!

Winnie is the star of the bestselling Winnie the Horse Gentler series that sold more than half a million copies and taught kids around the world about faith, kindness, and horse training. Winnie could ride horses before she could walk, but training them is another story. In this new series, eight-year-old Winnie learns the fine art of horse gentling from her horse wrangler mom as they work together to save the family ranch.

www.tyndalekids.com

Join twelve-year-old Winnie Willis and her friends—
both human and animal—on their adventures through
paddock and pasture as they learn about caring for
others, trusting God, and growing up.

Collect all eight Winnie the Horse Gentler books.
Or get the complete collection with the Barn Boxed Set!